SIRI *the Conquistador*

SIRI *the Conquistador*

by MARY STOLZ
Pictures by BENI MONTRESOR

HARPER & ROW, PUBLISHERS, NEW YORK AND EVANSTON

To that lover of small creatures,

my mother

SIRI *the Conquistador*

From the farthest corner of their tunnel beneath the floorboards, Asa and Rambo, storeroom mice, were regarding a nose at their mousehole.

"It isn't Siri's," Asa whispered. He quivered from tail to whisker-tip.

"Not unless he's grown a lot since yesterday," said Rambo. "And changed color," he added.

No, it was not the trim little black nose of their

old friend and enemy, Siri, now resident cat of Benn's Delicatessen. This nose was big and brown and eager, a snuffling, snooping horror at their mousehole.

"This is a terrible experience," Rambo said angrily, as if Asa might be tempted to disagree.

Asa was not.

"It's a dragon," he said hoarsely.

"How would a dragon get in a delicatessen?" Rambo demanded.

"I don't care how it got *in*," Asa wailed. "When is it going to get *out*, that's what I want to know."

They huddled together as the big snout wiggled from side to side, sniffing for them. Suddenly the nose disappeared, and two heavily clawed feet began to scrabble at their entrance. An anxious whining accompaniment echoed through the storeroom.

"Rambo," Asa said in a faint, brave voice. "You

don't have to remain at my side. Go on without me." He closed his eyes.

"Go on without you where?" Rambo said indignantly. "There's only one direction to go on in. Right toward that nose."

"Oh, I forgot," Asa said. He opened his eyes and looked around. Sure enough, they were backed against the wall. "And I always thought it was so roomy under here."

"I suppose," said Rambo, "any place seems roomy when there's nothing blocking the exit."

The assault seemed to go on forever . . . first the feet with dragonlike claws, then the nose, breathing heavily enough to stir the dust only inches from the cowering mice.

Then all at once nose and paws were gone and a terrible din in the storeroom ensued. There was yowling and yelping, punctuated by savage hisses,

followed by the sound of heavy paws retreating and a human voice that said, "There, there, Rowdy. Did the bad cat scare you?"

Barks, the slam of the storeroom door, a scornful sniff, and then silence.

"A dog," Asa said, curling his tail nervously. "It was a dog."

"We should have guessed," said Rambo. He sounded airy now, almost in command of himself. But he too curled his tail, first to one side, then to the other.

"Why should we have guessed, please?"

"Because this isn't the season for dragons," Rambo replied, as if he knew what he were talking about.

"Didn't you ever hear of things growing out of season?" Asa demanded.

When they were frightened, they tended to be a little cross with each other, a failing they shared with humans and other animals.

"Hey there, you two! Psst, psst . . . Are you there?" It was Siri at their doorway now, inquiring delicately into their well-being.

"Don't answer him," Rambo whispered.

"But, Rambo, he saved our lives."

"Not on purpose, I bet. Anyway, not really. We'd have been all right. Just a matter of keeping our heads."

"That's just what I was afraid we weren't going to do."

"Asa, you worry too much."

"There's no season on that either," said Asa. But with the dog gone, he was feeling better.

"Psst, psst . . . Asa! Rambo! Answer me . . . Are you all right?"

"Now, *there,*" said Asa to his brother. "He's concerned about us."

"Cats are always concerned about mice," Rambo pointed out. "It's their nature."

"Siri is not an ordinary cat," Asa said firmly.

"And he doesn't have an ordinary nature."

Rambo had to agree that Siri, the tiger cat, was far less given to natural prowling and hunting than he was to unnaturally long conversations. Give him a proper listener and he forgot his feline duties altogether. Give him *two* listeners . . . Well, Asa and Rambo had been audience to his tales for a long time now, and they had the run of the storeroom (except for the imported cheese) with Siri's blessing.

"Oh, my, oh, my," said Siri at the mousehole. "Oh, deary me. He must have frightened them to death. Oh, my poor little friends who lent me their ears so charmingly . . ."

"Rambo, this is *mean*," said Asa. He lifted his voice. "We're here, Siri. Don't worry."

"Heavens, *what* a relief," the cat cried out. "You have no idea how upset I've been. Come closer, and I'll tell you about it."

Asa and Rambo ran up the tunnel and stopped

8

a few inches from the entrance.

Siri (as he always did) said, "Why don't you come out here?"

"That's all right," the mice assured him. "We can hear every word you say from here."

"But it would be so much more convenient if we were all together."

"More convenient for whom?" said Rambo.

Unprepared to answer a question so bluntly put, Siri gave in (as he always did), and from their side of the mousehole Asa and Rambo listened to the cat, as he told them from his side about the advent of Rowdy, a dog.

"The size of a pony, I assure you," said Siri. "With the manners of a wild boar and a disposition like ground glass. He knocked over a stand of crackers in the shop, stole a roll of baloney, frightened a little boy up on the counter, and barked so much that Mr. Benn threatened to stuff a grapefruit in his mouth."

"Why didn't he?" Rambo asked.

"Maybe he couldn't find one," said Siri after a thoughtful pause.

"But how did he get in here to begin with?" Asa demanded.

"You may well ask," said Siri. "An excellent question and well put."

Asa preened himself a little at this praise.

"He's here," Siri went on, "by invitation. I gather he is the awful responsibility of Mrs. Benn's cousin, who is going on a trip to the Southwest and does not wish to take this—this—"

"Dragon," Rambo suggested.

"A dragon," said Siri, "has a certain poetry about him. This creature has not." Siri, who felt himself to have an excellent poetic grasp, delivered the criticism sharply.

Asa and Rambo had to agree that what they'd seen of Rowdy was not poetic.

"The cousin," Siri continued, "does not wish

to take–this *colossus* with her."

"Can't blame her for that," Rambo muttered.

"So he's staying here until she gets back."

"Eek!!" said Asa, as Rambo squeaked, "How long?"

"That's the question," said Siri glumly, settling down and curling his paws against his chest as if to comfort them. "Where's the Southwest?"

Asa and Rambo, who'd once made a sea voyage to a jungle and so might be considered travelers, had no idea where the Southwest was. They didn't know where the jungle was, either. They didn't even know where the delicatessen was. The only place they were sure of was their mousehole.

"So here we are," Siri grumbled. "Invaded by a vulgarian, with no idea when the invasion will be over. As that great poet Woolworth has said so well . . . *Dogs are too much with us, late and soon.*"

Asa, who'd once been friends with a library mouse, opened his mouth to say, "Wordsworth," but Rambo trod on his toe before the word was out.

"His *pride*," Rambo whispered. "You're always forgetting his pride."

"He's always forgetting it himself."

"That's his prerogative, not yours," Rambo said sternly.

"Besides, it's 'the *world* is too much with us, late and soon.' Not dogs," said Asa.

"Maybe the world right now *is* dogs to Siri. I know it feels like it to me. Siri?" Rambo said urgently.

"Yes, Rambo?"

"What are you going to do?"

Silence.

"Siri!" Asa called.

"Yes, Asa?"

"Once you said you'd leave any house where they brought a dog to live. You won't do that, will you?"

Silence again.

Side by side, the mouse brothers waited tensely. It was all terribly upsetting. That nose. Those

claws. That frightful din. And now Siri, not talking. All was awry, and the two little mice trembled for their future.

If Siri left, what would become of them? Mr.

and Mrs. Benn would surely get another cat—one that would behave just like a cat. No other cat in the world would be to them what Siri was . . . a natural enemy turned protector, a foe become friend, through the happy medium of words. What if Siri did insist on carrying the bulk of the conversation? It was still an exchange of views, a meeting of minds, working to the benefit of all.

But now here was this other party, enemy of cats and mice alike, and clearly limited as to conversation. What were they to do about him? Or, on the other—more important—hand, what was he going to do about them?

"Anyway," Rambo said loudly, hoping to goad Siri into speech, "anyway, that Rowdy is afraid of Siri. That much is plain."

"Afraid?" said Siri, his attention caught at last. "Of me? Whatever gives you such a notion?"

"Well, but Siri—we *heard* him. He yelped and

yowled and the person *said* you'd scared him."

"Oh, the person." Siri sniffed. "That was his owner. People who own dogs have no sense of proportion. No, abashed as I am to admit it, that creature terrified me. I had just come in here to pass the time of day with you two, and I ran into that–that *behemoth*. Oh, I knew he was somewhere about, having heard Mr. and Mrs. Benn talking over what it would be like to have a dog around– as if there were two sides to such a question–" He broke off and looked about edgily. "Where was I?"

"You were saying that you came in here to have a talk–" Rambo began, as Asa said, "You were telling us that the dog terrified you–"

Rambo glared at Asa, who refused to meet his eye. The important thing here was not what Siri had been doing but what he was going to do. How did he really feel about dogs? Siri was such a story-teller that it was hard to believe him when he boasted, but almost as hard to believe him when he didn't.

Asa had heard that the average cat was a match in a fight for the average dog, cats being quicker, sharper, and not subject to commands from their owners. A person could order a dog to stop fighting and the dog might very well do it, but whoever ordered a cat to do anything? Asa fancied that dogs, always expecting instructions from above, might be somewhat handicapped in arguments.

Against that was the knowledge that Siri simply was not the average cat. He hated the outdoors, did all his fighting in words, and spent most of his time conversing with a couple of mice. And he had left his first home when the threat of a dog arose.

Would he leave this one, too? That, so far as Asa was concerned, was the heart of the matter.

"Siri," he said again, "once you said you'd

never live in a house where they had a dog—"

"I did, didn't I?" said Siri. "Well, but that was in another house, and besides, this dog is temporary. Fear not, little ears, I shall remain."

"I think," said Rambo, "that even if you were afraid of the dog, he was afraid of you, too. I never heard such a carrying-on."

"Well, now, as I see it," Siri began happily, caring for nothing more than the opportunity to explain something, "as I see it—it was my appearance that undid him. When I'm alarmed, I really am a fearsome sight. Fur stands on end, tail gets like a great storm signal, back lifts up like the hump of doom. And then, of course, my voice sounds ghastly, even in my own ears. And sparks seem to fly around me. Oh, it's a horrid spectacle. The first time I caught sight of myself in a mirror I got in such a panic that I scared myself clear to the roof.

Took three firemen to get me down. And I still don't like coming upon myself unexpectedly in mirrors. Oh, yes, I can see why that–that *Goliath* was fearful. You'd be, too."

Knowing all too well how right he was, Asa and Rambo edged backward slightly in their tunnel.

"Temporary," Siri went on reflectively. "That's the key word. You can stand anything if you know it isn't going to last."

"But looked at in one way," Asa said, "everything is temporary. Temporary could be just this side of forever."

"There is nothing that requires us to look at it in that way," Siri said calmly. "We'll assume it to mean a short time. When she gets back from the Southwest–and no matter where it is, if she can get to it, she can get back again–he'll leave, and that will be that. Things will go on as before. Unless,

20

of course–" he added slowly, and then said, "but no, no. That's not possible. . . ."

"What's not possible?" said Asa and Rambo, their spirits, which had been lifting higher and higher, suddenly shooting downward. "Unless what, were you going to say?"

Siri stood up. "It's too silly. Doesn't bear thinking of."

"What doesn't?" asked the mice, miserably determined to know all.

"I was going to say, unless they get so fond of having a–a–" words failed him "–a *dog* around that they get one for themselves. But, as I say, that's silly. What would they *want* with a dog?"

"What, indeed?" said Rambo bravely, and Asa echoed, "Silly, of course."

"Adieu, you two," said Siri, who'd been sitting next to some wild French forest strawberries. He went off on his soundless feet, and when he was quite gone, Asa and Rambo came out in the store-room.

At first they could only nibble worriedly at some broken crackers near the mousehole. But presently Asa found a filbert. Now, if there was one thing he knew about a worry it was that you could always find it where you'd left it. A filbert, on the other hand, was sure to be gone. So he dropped the worry and attended to the nut.

Rambo dared himself to try a bit of fig, and by the time he'd taken the dare and then quickly swallowed some cheddar to forget that he had, he'd forgotten Rowdy also.

They sampled the treasures of the storeroom (honorably passing up the imported cheese, as they had promised Siri). Then they played tag. . . .

Over dark gold cans of Colombian coffee, wooden chests of candied fruit from Eastern ba-zaars, crates of white endives from Belgium, and little forest strawberries from France, through and around tins of Holland biscuits and Portuguese sardines they raced and scampered. The air of the storeroom was warm, rich with hints of ginger, cardamom, and rosemary, with the scent of salami and pastrami and crisp-crusted breads, with the briny tang of pickles, and boxes that had crossed the ocean in sea-salted holds.

Oh, the storeroom in which they played was a very heaven of odor and taste and security. . . .

At length they flung themselves down beside a pyramid of Swiss preserves. Rambo was the triumphant winner and he panted accordingly. Asa panted, too, and wondered how it was that with only two of them playing, he was always It. But then he thought how lucky a mouse he was to have such a small bewilderment his only problem—

And that recalled the worry he'd dropped in favor of a filbert. He had come full circle.

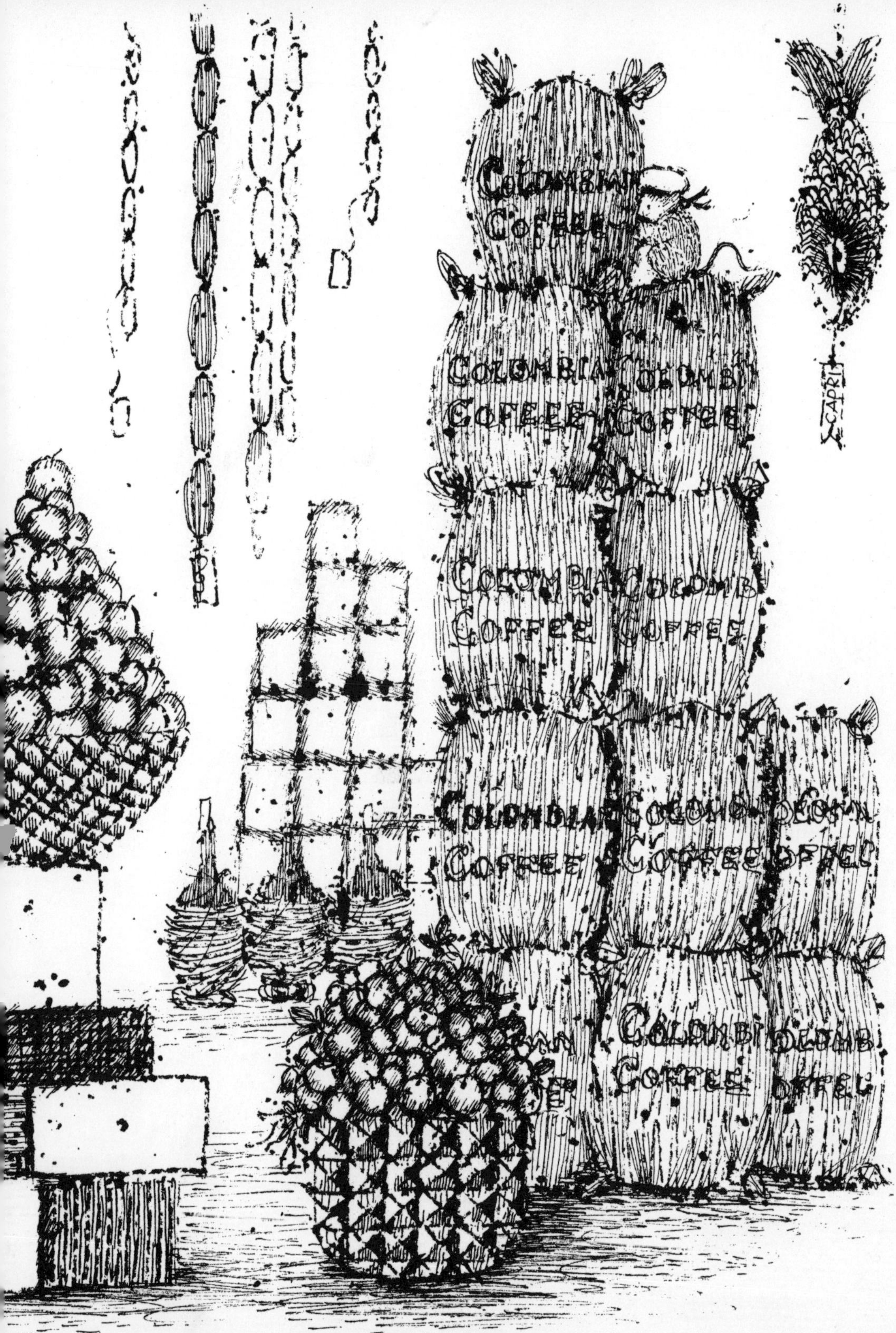
COLOMBIA COFFEE
CAPRI

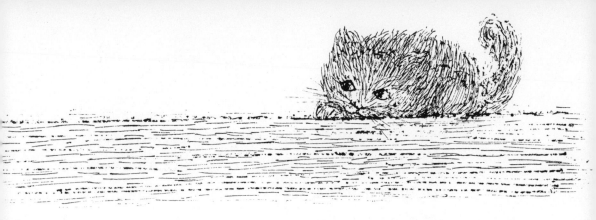

"Rambo," he said. "I hope–that is, wouldn't it be awful if–I mean, I *do* hope we never have to leave here."

"Oh, stop," said Rambo faintly. He was a brave mouse who did not always feel equal to his own courage.

Time passed.

Sometimes Rowdy, the dog, found his way into the storeroom, and each time he came, Asa and Rambo fled to the end of their tunnel and crouched there, atremble, wondering if this time their end

had come. But Mr. and Mrs. Benn always got him quickly out, as he had a heavy tail and a way of wagging it that sent olives rolling into corners and left the floor full of broken glass.

Siri didn't come around as often as before. "I've taken to living on top of things," he explained one day during a brief visit.

"On top of what things?" Asa asked.

"Just about anything. Doors, bureaus, even the porch roof. I sort of feel safer off the ground. Besides, I've discovered that that—that *monster* doesn't like to find me staring down at him from various perches."

"Unaccountable," said Rambo, and shivered.

"Thinks, probably, that I'll drop on him," Siri continued cheerfully. "Not that I will. Not that I *couldn't.*"

"Oh, no, Siri," said the mice. "That is, of course you could."

"I just prefer not to be in such close contact with

him," the cat elaborated. *"Let this cup pass from me,* said the psalmist."

"Very understandable," Rambo assured him, and Siri went off, his proud tail high, while Asa explained to Rambo that the quotation was actually from the New Testament.

"The Southwest," Rambo said to Asa one day, "must be at the other end of the world."

"Or else the person likes it and has decided to take up residence."

Rambo was outraged. "Well, if that's the case," he squeaked, "why doesn't she send for her *dog?* Do these people think our hospitality has no limits?"

"They probably don't think about our hospitality at all," Asa mused. "I mean, if they did, wouldn't Siri be in a pretty pickle?"

Rambo fell silent.

They were in their tunnel, tails curled together

for comfort against these trying times. Suddenly they heard the soft footfall of Siri in the storeroom.

"Hey, there," said the cat. "Come out and hear what I've been thinking."

"Thank you, Siri," they said politely. "We'll stay here and listen."

"Oh, very well," said Siri, this time not even troubling to coax. He settled down beside the mousehole, toyed with a filbert for a few moments, then said, "Catch," and shot it neatly through their doorway into Asa's paws.

"Wonder how I happened to miss that one," Asa said. But he didn't feel like eating.

"Well?" said Rambo to the cat.

"Well, what?"

"You said you were going to tell us what you've been thinking."

Siri did not answer immediately. He licked a paw disconsolately, studied the twitching tip of his tail as though wondering why it twitched, and then stared around the storeroom.

More and more uneasy, the mice waited.

"It's this way," Siri said at last. "I've been thinking–"

"Yes, Siri?" they encouraged when he stopped again.

"I've been thinking that in their greedy, grasping, ill-behaved way–perhaps dogs aren't too bad."

A shock of silence followed this statement. The mouse brothers, nose to nose, stared into each other's eyes.

"What does that mean?" Asa whispered.

"It probably means she isn't coming back from the Southwest," Rambo decided gloomily.

"Not at all," said Siri. "She just came and took him away. Oh, it was enough to make a cat laugh, let me tell you. The carryings-on. The shrieking and patting and whimpering and barking. *Oh, how*

I've missed you, and *Oh, do you love me?* Really
. . . dogs." The cat sniffed. "So insecure."

"I'm feeling a little insecure myself," said
Rambo.

"But, Siri," Asa said loudly, "if he's gone, why
do you start finding reasons to like him now? I
suggest that we just forget the whole experience."

"Because," said Siri in an ominous tone, "it has
come to pass."

"What has?" they squeaked.

"They–Mr. and Mrs. Benn–have decided to get
–to get–"

"To get a dog?" Rambo gulped.

"For themselves?" Asa gasped.

"To live here?" they cried out in despair.

"That's the way it is," said Siri. "He's coming
in a couple of days. His name," the cat went on in
a hollow voice, "is Maximilian."

32

"Oh, my, oh, my," breathed Rambo, stunned.

Asa could not speak at all. His heart had taken a sudden skid and his voice went along.

Word-conscious as they all were, the name *Maximilian* plunged them in gloom. It was so long, so strong, so emperorlike.

"He'll be worse than Portman," Rambo guessed.

Portman had been the fierce Mouse-at-Large in the house they'd lived in before coming to the delicatessen. They had left that house, unable to tolerate Portman's tyranny. But if a mouse named Portman could be overbearing and dictatorial, what would a dog named Maximilian be?

"What are we going to do?" Rambo moaned.

"Shall we have to run away again?" Asa sobbed.

"I always said," Siri began, "that no place was big enough for me and a dog, too—"

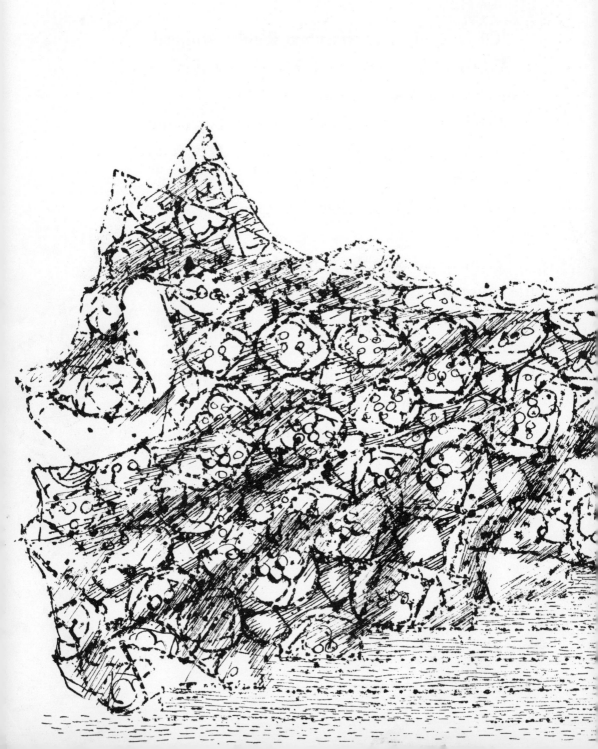

MAXIMILIAN

"Yes, Siri. We know. Of course, if you go, we'll go, too," Rambo said. "Except I can't think where."

"Well," said Siri, his voice gathering strength, "I have changed my mind." He eyed the two mice, who in their fascination had crept almost out of the mousehole. "We are not going."

"We aren't?" they breathed.

"We are not."

"What are we going to do instead?" Rambo asked. He had visions of never getting out of the tunnel again, of relying on Siri's kindness (pretty good) and Siri's memory (not good) to send them provisions from time to time. No more games of tag in the warmth and fragrance of the storeroom. No more happy naps beside the Roquefort—

"I look at it this way," Siri continued in his explanatory tone, the one that meant he was digging in for a good long talk. "I'm too old to keep on

36

running. I just haven't the heart for it any more. Or the strength," he added with sad candor. "And you two are too young. So . . . we can't run."

"What can we do?" Asa asked.

"Coexist," said Siri.

Another silence, and then Rambo asked his brother, "Do you know what that means?" Asa shook his head.

Siri undertook to explain. "In its broadest sense," he said, "it means to live in conjunction with, or at the same time as, another. It is in that broad sense that one might say we three dwell together. Or coexist." He blinked and stroked a whisker. "In another, narrower, sense, it means to get along with the enemy. With Maximilian we shall observe it in its narrow sense."

"What sense will he observe it in?" Asa asked.

"Asa," said Siri sternly, "sometimes I detect in you a tendency to carp."

37

"Sorry," said Asa. "I was just wondering."

"Well, don't. I have everything under control. Now . . . the minute this Maximilian arrives, I shall get on top of something, and then I shall stare down at him, like this—"

The two mice looked up and then flung themselves backward into the tunnel. Even knowing him as they did, Siri presented a terrible aspect. His yellow eyes were huge and hot as furnaces, his lips curled upward, baring slender teeth, his whiskers spiked out stiffly, and his fur was all on end.

"Now," said Siri, fur and whiskers smoothing, eyes growing mild again, "now, if you were Maximilian and you found me staring at you like that from the top of a door, and I said, '*Maximilian, you will coexist with me and my friends or I'll know the reason why,*' what would you do?"

"Coexist as fast as possible," said Asa.

38

"I wouldn't want to know the reason why," Rambo said, still weak from that fearful vision.

"Then that's all settled," said Siri. "First I'll terrify him, then we'll coexist. Oh, and we *ought* to try to find a few good points in him. No simple matter with a dog, but we'll do what we can."

He sounded a lot more confident than any of them felt, but no one was going to admit it.

"Did I ever tell you," Siri went on, firmly changing the subject, "about the time I fought that enormous water rat and ran him right into the bay? Well . . . it was shortly after daybreak, and I was coming home from a night's fencing–"

He went on happily, and the two mice listened with considerable interest. They did not know whether he'd told them the story before or not, as he never told anything twice in the same fashion. It made him a most entertaining speaker. The

39

fight, the water rat, and the bay got bigger and bigger as the story progressed, and squeaks from the mice did nothing to diminish them.

When that and yet one more stimulating tale were finished, Siri rose to take his leave. "All settled," he said again, and then, as he went through the storeroom door, "I *wish* I didn't keep remembering the poet's warning—*The best-laid schemes o' cats an' mice gang aft agley . . .*"

"Misquoting, always misquoting," said Asa.

"*Gang aft agley,*" Rambo said pensively. "What does that mean, Asa?"

Asa said with reluctance, "I expect it means, *Often go wrong.*"

"Just about what I thought." Rambo sighed.

"Rambo, there's something we've overlooked."

Rambo turned his head away, as if he'd rather not know, but Asa persisted, "Rambo, Siri said if we were Maximilian and a cat looked at us like

that, what would we do, and we agreed that we'd
do whatever we were told—"

"Well, what's wrong with that?" Rambo said
testily.

"Well, Rambo . . . we *aren't* Maximilian."

Rambo inched away from his brother and decided that Siri was right. Asa had a tendency to
carp.

Two days later the mice were resting in a broad
band of sunlight lying across the storeroom windowsill. They had eaten well and played hard.
Now it was so peaceful in the dust-dancing after-
noon light, with no sound but that of some dreamy
bees in the lilac bush outside, that the mouse
brothers had forgotten care.

Rambo was lost in heroic visions. He saw the
jungle, and tigers, and himself at the prow of a
flying ship.

Asa drowsed and wondered if to be a bee in a flower was as fine a thing as to be a mouse on a sunny windowsill, watching the bee at work.

Suddenly they heard a yelping from the delicatessen. They flashed back to the tunnel, hearts thumping, tails curling nervously from side to side, whiskers quivering, dreams and fancies gone like smoke.

It seemed ages that they waited, hoping for news from Siri. Had he made it to a door top? Had he flared and glared and growled in a manner sufficient to impress a dog named Maximilian? Suppose Maximilian didn't know what coexistence meant? Would he wait for an explanation, or would he just run Siri out of the house? Siri was shocking in appearance when he put his mind to it, but would his mind obey, or would it just remember that he was afraid of dogs?

Which would it be? Siri the mask of horror

terrifying Maximilian or Siri forgetting everything except how to run away from a dog?

They waited . . . and waited . . . and waited. . . .

When the sun had left the windowsill and crept across the floor, up the wall, and away, they heard, at length, paws at the storeroom door, a skirmish and murmur, the click-click-clack of light claws, and then Siri's voice at the mousehole.

"Asa! Rambo! Come to the door, will you? I would like you to meet Maximilian, from Mexico."

The two mice crept warily to their entrance and stared out. Their eyes got wider and wider, their mouths fell open.

Siri smiled and smirked at the side of Maximilian from Mexico.

"Why, he looks something like Portman," Asa whispered. "Unless Portman's a little bigger."

Indeed, Maximilian was almost mouse-sized.

He had huge popping eyes, flaring ears, the thin-
nest little body, and legs like lilac twigs. He
pranced uneasily on his tiny paws and stared and
stared at Siri, as if the cat were his father.

"You know," said Rambo, "if he held his
breath, he could get *in* here."

"You will be interested to know, I know," said
Siri, "that Maximilian is a Chihuahua and comes
of an ancient family, antedating, I understand, even
the Aztec civilization–"

"What's he talking about?" Rambo asked his
brother.

"Babbling with relief, I think," said Asa.

"Maxie's a puppy," Siri went on patronizingly.
"He's going to grow at least another inch."

"That should keep him out of here, at any rate,"
Rambo said.

"Now, now," said Siri. "We must be kind to
our visitor."

"Visitor?" said Asa. "You mean he's going away again?"

"No, no," Siri said a bit tartly. "I mean he's from a foreign land. That makes him a visitor, just at first. Of course," he added kindly to the little dog, "in no time you'll be right at home."

Maximilian looked unconvinced.

"Are we still going to coexist with him?" Asa asked.

"Of course, of course," said Siri.

"In the narrow sense?" asked Rambo.

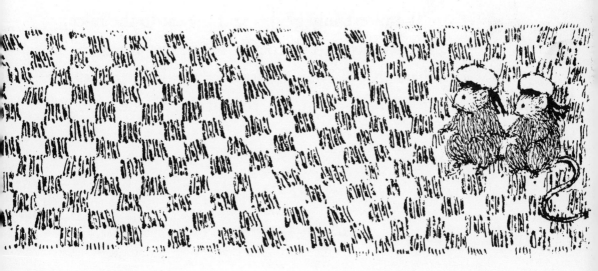

"In the broad," Siri decided comfortably. He looked at the puppy. "After all, the morsel isn't big enough to be a foe, now is he?"

Even Asa and Rambo had to admit that silent, skinny, woeful-eyed Maximilian made a pretty small enemy. He blinked at the two mice as they studied him and then fastened his gaze again on Siri, as if upon a savior.

Siri's purr was loud in the dim and spicy storeroom. It was truly his day of triumph. Two intelligent mice with whom to exchange literary views and discuss world events (or stories about them, which in a sense came to the same thing)—and now a dog to be unafraid of.

"I am certainly glad," said the cat to the mice, "that we decided to coexist *before* we saw Maximilian—that is, Maxie. Now we need never doubt our courage again. So reassuring. Come along,

Maxie . . . I'll show you around the garden." As they started off, the mice heard him saying, "Do you know that beautiful poem of Woolworth's which begins—*Come into the garden, Max, for the black bat, night, has flown—?*"

"Siri's cup certainly runneth over," said Asa.

"I can hear it splash from here," Rambo replied. He called out, "Good-bye, Siri. Good-bye, Maximilian. . . ."

"*Adios, amigos,*" said Siri as he went around the corner.

Asa and Rambo sighed and decided to go to bed.

"Do you suppose," Asa asked drowsily, "that Siri is right?"

"About what?"

"About never needing to doubt our courage again?"

"Well," said Rambo after a pause, "why do we

have to think about it at all? We were courageous *that* time. If an occasion to be brave arises again— well, we'll see what happens."

"It isn't easy to be a mouse," said Asa.

"No. No, it isn't. But I expect," Rambo mused, "that it isn't easy to be a cat, either. Or a dog. Maybe it isn't easy to be a person."

"Oh, you go too far," said Asa.

"I'm not sure," Rambo replied darkly, but since he really didn't know anything about it at all, he got back to mice. "What it comes to, Asa—speaking as a mouse, you understand—is that it's a very good thing to be sure of yourself. But not too sure. Do you agree?"

"*Si, amigo,*" said Asa, closing his eyes. "I agree."

51

Format by Jean Krulis

Set in Linotype Granjon

Composed and bound by American Book–Stratford Press

Printed by Murray Printing Co.

HARPER & ROW, PUBLISHERS, INCORPORATED